The
Mouse
Couple

The Mouse Couple

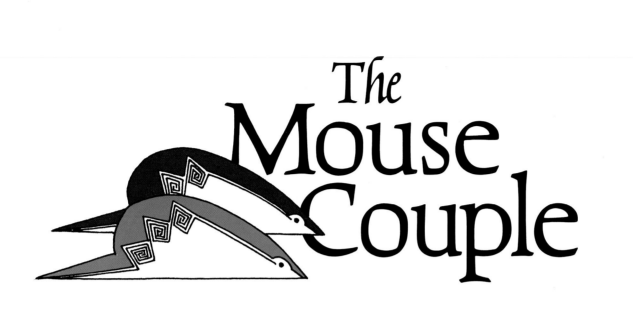

A Hopi Folktale

Retold by Ekkehart Malotki, Illustrated by Michael Lacapa

NORTHLAND PUBLISHING

FIRST EDITION

Second Printing 1990

ISBN-0-87358-473-2

Library of Congress Catalog Card Number 88-60916

Composed in the United States of America

Library of Congress Cataloging-in-Publication Data
Malotki, Ekkehart
The mouse couple: a Hopi folktale / retold by Ekkehart Malotki;
illustrated by Michael Lacapa.—1st ed.
pp.64   cm.
Summary: A mouse couple, in search of the mightiest husband for
their daughter, approach the sun, the clouds, the wind, and a butte,
before the unexpected victor finally appears.
ISBN 0-87358-473-2: $14.95
1. Hopi Indians—Legends. 2. Indians of North America—Arizona—
Legends.[1. Hopi Indians—Legends. 2. Indians of North America—
Legends. 3. Mice—Folklore. 4. Marriage—Folklore.] I. Lacapa,
Michael, ill. II. Title.
E99.H7M3445 1988
398.2′08997—dc19
88-60916
CIP
AC

Manufactured in Hong Kong

8-90/5M/0314

To all
The suns, clouds, winds, buttes,
Mice, and little girls
In the galaxy.

Aliksa'i (LISTEN)

P EOPLE LIVED IN VILLAGES THROUGHOUT THE LAND.
And since mice live just about anywhere that
humans do, a pair of them, husband and wife, also
lived at a place just east of Pavi'ovi. Unfortunately,
they had not been blessed with children, and were
afraid that they would have no one to care for them in
their old age. The husband and wife were in their middle
years, and old age seemed to be approaching fast. Mouse
constantly worried, and pictured what it might be like
in old age without any children, so one morning during
breakfast he said to his wife, "I've been troubled about
something."

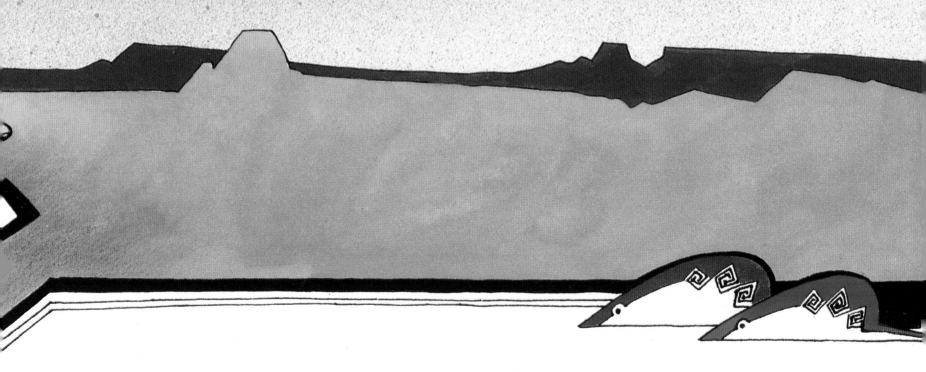

"What is it?" his wife asked.

"Yes, well, we're getting older every day and we don't have a daughter, or even a son for that matter, who is our own flesh and blood," he explained. "We have no one to take care of us when we get old. Because of this, I keep thinking how good it would be if someone happened to give us a child to tend to our needs."

"Yes, perhaps so," replied his wife. "I've been having the same kind of thoughts, but kept them to myself until now. We've obviously been thinking along the same lines, but how will we find a child?"

"I believe there's only one way," Mouse said. "Prayer is the only answer. From today on we'll go out to pray every morning and concentrate on one purpose: finding a child. Perhaps someone will then have pity on us and grant us an infant of our own. If we're fortunate, perhaps the child will be a girl who can learn to cook for us."

"Yes, indeed," his wife readily agreed.

At about this time, winter was approaching and it was the time of year when people were harvesting and storing

2

their crops. As they had decided, the mouse couple went out every morning and prayed to the rising sun for a child. Morning after morning they prayed, always placing some prayer feathers on the ground. So sincere were they in their desire for an infant that they also prayed during the nights, which were growing steadily colder and colder.

In this manner they prayed, morning and night, on into the middle of winter as the people of days past used to do during this season, asking for abundant snow and rainfall. All winter long they continued to pray.

Then one morning before dawn, the mouse couple were about to go out and perform their daily observance when they heard a noise, like the crying of an infant. It seemed to be coming from just outside their home. Mouse said to his wife, "Listen! It sounds like a baby crying. I wonder who would have a child out in weather like this; it's freezing out there. It's probably crying from the cold. I'll go take a look and see."

When he emerged from his hole, snow blanketed the ground. It was as deep as his knee, perhaps deeper, and

more snow was falling. He could see nothing, so he went back inside and called to his wife, "Get up. Let's go out and look around. I think someone is out there with a child. We should find them and bring them in so the child can warm up. It's freezing out there, there's a thick layer of snow on the ground, and more is falling."

Again the cries came. Now the mouse wife got out of bed and the two of them went out into the snow together

to look for the source of the cries. There was no doubt now; somewhere a child was really screaming. The mouse couple peered intently through the falling snow, but there was no sign of anyone. The infant let out another piercing howl, and lo and behold, there was a baby mouse, right at the edge of their hole! The poor thing was all huddled up and shivering as it lay there. "There it is, I see it now!" Mouse exclaimed.

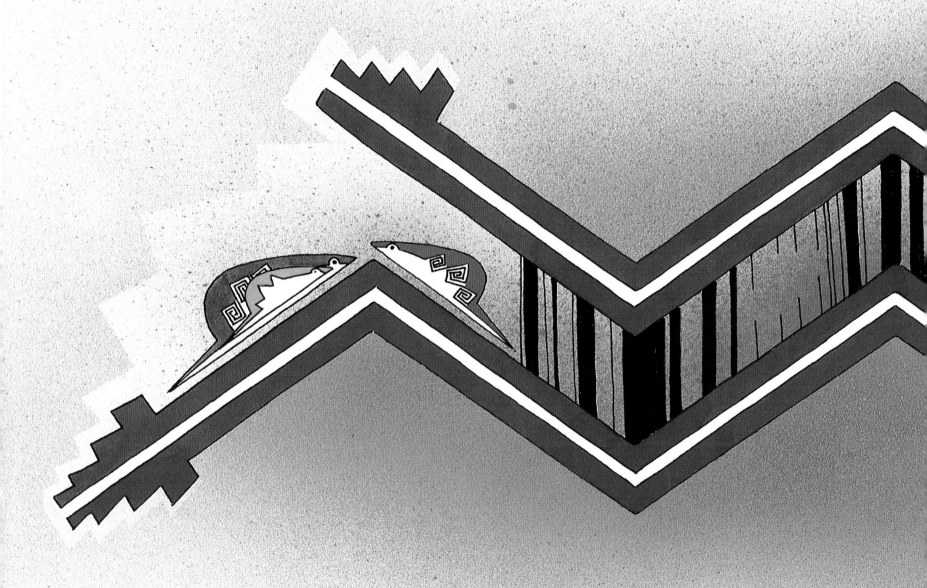

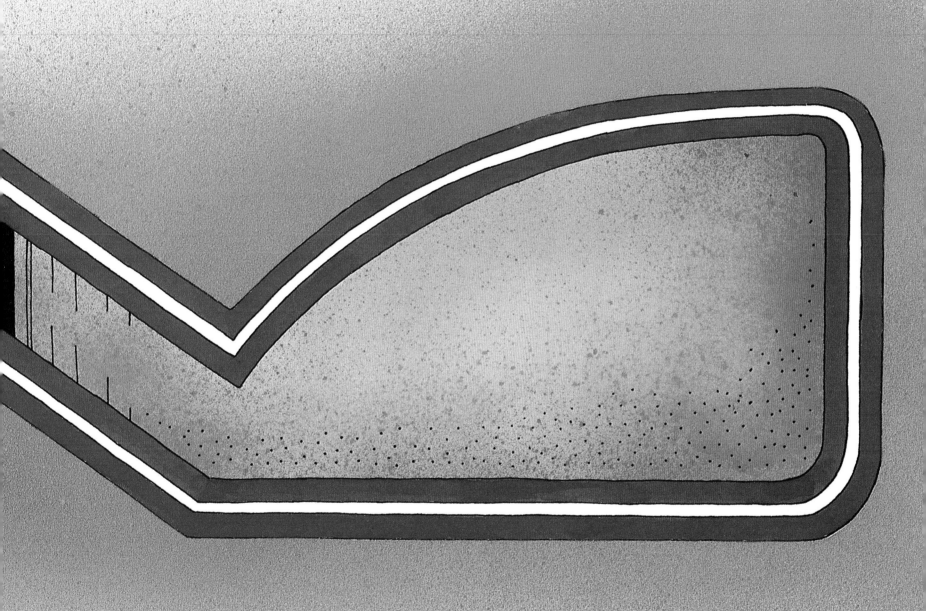

"Oh, how awful!" said his wife, in anguish. "Who would leave such a poor little thing like you out here in the cold?" She picked the child up and carried it quickly inside, followed by Mouse. Right away she found a blanket and bundled it up snugly. "Stoke the fire," she bade her husband. "This poor little creature must be chilled to the bone."

Mouse stirred the glowing embers, and when the flames sprung up, his wife took the infant over to the fireplace and warmed it. After she was sure it was thoroughly warm and comfortable, she began to feed it. Of course, it is the habit of mice to make off with corn and other human food, which they store for themselves to live on during the cold winter months. So, it was some of this food—finely ground baked sweet corn—which she moistened and put into the baby's mouth. Soon the baby was full and quickly fell into a deep sleep. When the wife took a closer look at the child, she discovered that it was a girl. The mouse couple was overjoyed, and Mouse cried, "Thanks, thanks, it looks like we have been given a child!"

From that day on the mouse couple took care of the

8

child, looking forward to the future when she would take care of them. Always in their minds was the fear that the child's mother had abandoned her near the mouse couple's hole shortly after birth, and would come back some day and reclaim her. They kept their ears open for any rumors, but not a word was going around as to how the child got there. Finally, they concluded that someone with faith in them had sent the child in answer to their prayers, and so they continued to raise her with free minds.

The years passed, and the girl soon reached the age where she was able to perform all sorts of tasks. The mouse wife taught her to cook and the girl grew up knowing how to prepare a variety of dishes.

And so the mouse couple and their daughter lived happily and contentedly at their home near Pavi'ovi. The father took great delight in the girl and all the delicious dishes she cooked for him. Because he regarded her so highly, he wanted the best for her and his mind was set on finding just the right suitor for her.

Once, as the three of them were having a meal, Mouse

spoke to his daughter: "My child," he said.

"Yes, father" she asked.

"I'm really delighted with you," said Mouse. "You know how to cook every kind of dish there is. You keep our home in order. And now that you are near the age when suitors will come calling, I've been thinking that we wouldn't want to give you up to just anyone. I want a husband of importance and high status for you."

"I see," she replied. "Of course that's up to you. Perhaps you've got someone in mind for me?"

"No," answered Mouse, "but I intend to go looking."

"All right," his daughter said. "When will you leave?"

"In four days. You are now fully grown and mature. Other girls of your age are already getting married," said Mouse. "It is time that I went."

"Very well. In that case I'll prepare some journey food for you. Will you be traveling far?"

"Yes, I will," said Mouse, "please go ahead and do that."

So the girl busied herself preparing food for Mouse's journey. When the third day arrived, she said to him, "It is

10

nearly time for you to leave."

"Yes, that's right," her father answered. "I'll be leaving early tomorrow morning."

"In which direction will you go?" she asked.

Mouse replied, "I'll be going east from here."

Dawn was just breaking the next morning as the girl readied her father's food and other supplies for the journey. Mouse rose early also, and after a few nibbles of breakfast, he shouldered his journey food, went out from his hole, and started off toward the East.

He had not reached his destination when evening fell, so he stopped and made camp, ate his supper, and bedded down for the night. The next morning while it was still dark, he arose and continued on his way. The grey light of dawn had not yet appeared when he came upon a kiva, an underground chamber, and began to enter. As he did so, a voice came from within, shouting, "I hear you up there stranger, come on in!"

Mouse entered the kiva. Once inside, he saw a young man who was in the process of putting on some beautiful clothes

11

and painting himself with brilliant colors. He stopped dressing and greeted Mouse heartily. "Have a seat, stranger! There is not much time left, and I must leave soon. That is why I was dressing when you came in. I'm sorry, but I won't have time to smoke with you." When Mouse saw the glorious youth and heard him speak, he knew that he was the one he had come seeking—the Sun.

"Is that so?" said Mouse. "That's too bad. I've come a long way especially to see you."

"Well, it does appear that you have some urgent matter on your mind," said the Sun youth.

"Yes, that's true. You see, I have a daughter who is now grown up. She is a very good cook and knows how to keep a house clean. She's of marriageable age and being a woman of many talents, I won't give her up to just anyone that comes along. It is my deep desire to have the best for her, and that's why I have sought you out here, for I'm sure there is no being greater than you."

"Is that right? Well thank you, thank you very much indeed!" exclaimed the youth. "So that's your reason for being here. It is true that every day I rise to keep the earth and all its creatures warm, as I soon must do once again. And yes, in summer I heat the earth and cause plants to sprout and grow. However, I must confess that I am really not the important one that you seek. That distinction must belong to the Clouds. Upon rising, I do indeed travel the sky above you, but when the rain clouds gather they spread out and form such a dense layer below me that my rays cannot pierce them. For this reason I believe that they must be the most important ones of all. I suggest that you go see them."

15

"Very well," said Mouse, "I will."

Sun continued, "Just head over that mountain range to the West of here and you will find them."

When Mouse came out of the kiva, he followed the instructions given to him by the Sun youth and trotted steadily off toward the West. Soon it became obvious to him that he was heading towards *Nuvatukya'ovi*, the San Francisco Peaks. As he neared Nuvatukya'ovi, the base of the mountains stretched out, green and beautiful. All around him, the fields were in full bloom and dew clung to the petals of flowers and blades of grass. Abundant green, growing things surrounded him.

Nearby, fully grown muskmelons, watermelons, and other crops lay in beautifully cultivated fields. Gentle rain settled on them as he watched, wondering who could be tending such fields.

Once again, he became aware that there was a kiva nearby, and cautiously he climbed to its rooftop. He had barely set foot on it, when a voice from within invited him inside. "I hear you up there, stranger. Don't be shy, come in, come in!" So Mouse entered the kiva, and when he reached the bottom of the entrance ladder and his eyes became accustomed to the kiva light, he noticed that there were people living there, a great many of them in fact. Men both young and old, women, young girls, children—all were living in this underground chamber. Standing to the east of the kiva ladder, he looked around. Although these people looked like humans, there was something about their appearance that made them seem very powerful. Along the east and west walls of the kiva, on beams hanging from the ceiling, were lightning bolt weapons and a great number of water canteens.

It was then that he realized that he must be in the kiva of the Clouds. Right at that time, all the inhabitants of the kiva welcomed him, and the Cloud leader, the eldest of those assembled there, beckoned him over, saying "All

right, come over here to me and have a seat." Mouse did as he was bidden and moved toward the firepit. There he sat down next to the Cloud leader, who offered him his pipe, and the two began to smoke silently. When the two had finished their ritual smoking, the Cloud leader began to speak to Mouse. "All right, I can only think that you have some very important reason for coming here to this place. No other stranger has ever before entered our home, but sure enough, you are right here before me. That makes me very curious."

"Well, yes, certainly I can understand your curiosity," said Mouse, "and I will tell you why I have come here all the way from my home at a place near Pavi'ovi. My wife and I have a daughter. She has grown up and it is now time for her to take a husband. I have come all this way, looking for a suitable one for her. It can't be just anyone. You see, my daughter is not like other girls. She knows how to prepare every kind of food, how to keep a home clean and attractive, and we never have to coax her into doing things—she does them on her own. She never puts off her tasks, and

always keeps busy. Therefore, perhaps you can understand that I don't want to give her up to just anyone.

"So, I went to the East first and sought out the Sun, he who travels above us and takes care of us at the same time, he who gives warmth to us as well as to the earth we live on. Because he provides these important things for us, I figured that he would be the best husband I could find for my daughter, and so I went looking for him first and told him this. I thought of giving my daughter to him, but apparently this cannot be. As the Sun himself told me, 'Granted, I travel across the sky above you and give you warmth, and during the warm season I provide heat for your crops so they will grow and mature. Because of my warmth, the earth blooms with flowers and grass becomes green every year.'

"This sort of power had been my reason for coming to him in the first place. But then the Sun conceded that he was not the highest being, as I had thought. He said, 'I have these powers, it is true, but I cannot overpower them,' meaning you, the Clouds. He suggested that you were the

real leaders of all, that you might be at the very zenith.
For though he indeed rises and travels above us, as soon as
you Clouds appear, to bring rain and spread yourselves out,
massing beneath him in the sky, he is hidden. When you
do this, his rays cannot penetrate to the ground and in this
way, you might be said to prevail over him. For this reason, he
believes that it is really you Clouds who are the most
powerful beings in existence. Therefore, I believe one of
you should marry my daughter. This was the Sun's proposal
and so he sent me here to you," Mouse said.

"Is that so? Very well, thank you indeed," exclaimed the
Cloud chief. He was elated at the high esteem in which
Mouse and the Sun apparently held him and his people. "But
I'm afraid that I too have to tell you that we may not be
so prominent as you think. What the Sun said is certainly true;
when we gather to make rain, we do form a thick mass
beneath him. We do this in response to the deepest desires
and heartfelt wishes of the humans. All the way to the
horizon we form pools of water with our moisture, and the
earth becomes beautifully green. The thirsty crops revive

and stand strong. Our moisture allows their growing shoots to mature and produce fruit which the humans and small animals then eat. But in truth I must say that we Clouds are not of the highest rank, and none of us is fit as a husband for your daughter. I believe that the cold North Winds surpass us. Let me tell you why.

"It's true, of course, that we come together powerfully when we gather to make rain. Nevertheless, at times the North Winds will not let us by when we come up against them. They blow so hard that we can't overcome them. They treat us terribly and scatter us all over the sky, exceeding our power with theirs. That's why none of us here is right for your daughter. Therefore, I must urge you to seek out the North Winds."

Disappointed, Mouse said, "That's too bad. I surely didn't want as a son-in-law anyone as disagreeable and unruly as one of the North Winds, but if you recommend it, I will go to them all the same."

Reluctantly, Mouse came out of the Cloud kiva and made his way North. After quite a long while, he felt a

stiff breeze on his face, and saw that he was nearing a canyon.
As he got nearer to the canyon, the breeze grew stronger
and stronger. When he finally reached the canyon rim, the
wind howled and blew with such force that it thrust him
backwards, and he had no choice but to stop where he was
and fall to the ground. He crept to the edge on his stomach
and peered down into the depths of the canyon. Pulsating
gusts of wind beat against him so that he could hardly see, but
much to his amazement, at the bottom of the canyon stood
another kiva. He thought this must be the home of the
North Winds.

27

He began to make his way down into the canyon, the wind beating against him as he clambered among the rocks. Time and again the wind would overwhelm him, and he would have to rest before going on. When he finally arrived at the kiva site, he was exhausted and paused to rest once more before climbing up on top of the kiva. No sooner had he climbed to the top than a call came from inside, welcoming him. "Don't hesitate up there stranger, come in! You are welcome!"

Mouse did as he was bidden, and entered the kiva. As he stepped off the last rung of the kiva ladder, he looked around at the occupants and was shocked to see how grotesque they were. Their hair was especially awful. It was a tangled mess, sticking out in every direction. The interior of the kiva was also a shambles, so that the kiva and its occupants together presented a completely disheveled appearance.

Then the leader of the North Winds spoke to him. "Have a seat, stranger. You must have some purpose for coming here to the depths of this canyon."

Unlike the Cloud chief, however, he did not offer Mouse a smoke, so Mouse answered right away, "Yes indeed, I came here to seek you out."

"All right," said the leader of the North Winds, "I can see that you have something important on your mind."

"Yes, you're right. You see, I have a daughter," began Mouse. "She can prepare any kind of dish there is. She is never lazy; in fact, she is very industrious and diligent. She never fails to do a woman's chores, and my wife and I delight in her greatly. Because of this, I don't want just an ordinary husband for her. I want someone of the highest standing.

"I first sought the Sun," Mouse continued. "Because of his brightness and power, I reasoned that he is the highest. But when I arrived at his home, he told me that this was not so." With that, Mouse gave the leader of the North Winds an account of what the Sun had said. "The Sun then sent me to the high mountains south of here, where I would find the Cloud people, who he said were greater than he. I told them the same story and they also claimed not to be the highest in standing. They sent me here, so perhaps it's you I

29

am looking for. I am looking for someone to marry my daughter, and that is the purpose of all my travels," concluded Mouse. "The Cloud chief told me that no one can get the better of you, and that is why I am here."

"Yes," the leader of the North Winds replied, "it may seem that there is no one more powerful than us, but I'm sorry to tell you that we are not the supreme ones either. It is indeed our nature to be powerful, and when we all come together we are a furious and irresistible force. We storm about, blowing over the strong walls of houses and upsetting even the pine and cottonwood trees, with their roots deep in the earth. Nothing dominates us. In that sense, the Cloud chief told you the truth."

The North Wind leader went on. "But I must tell you that we're not first among all powers. That position, I suspect, belongs to the Butte. I believe he must exceed all others, for nothing can harm him. Nothing has ever been able to topple him, not even we mighty North Winds. We cannot move him even the tiniest distance. He stands as he always has, unmoveable and rooted in the land. There is no use for us

33

to even try. That's why I believe you should approach him."

When Mouse heard this he was greatly relieved. He had not been happy at the prospect of one of the North Winds, with his tousled hair and generally wild appearance, marrying his daughter. He was glad when the leader of the North Winds said, "So, then, I recommend that you go visit the Butte and see what he has to say."

So Mouse left the kiva of the North Winds and began to make his way out of the canyon. Once again he was buffeted by ferocious winds as he climbed, but finally he made it. He headed for a point south of Songoopavi, and from there toward the buttes standing south of this village.

When he had arrived there, he saw no one that he could speak to. He stood there quite aimlessly for some time. Then suddenly a voice asked, "Who is that walking about?"

Mouse looked up, straining to see where the voice might have come from, but saw nothing. "I wonder where that voice came from?" he asked himself.

When the Butte, who had been right there in front of him all the time, realized how bewildered Mouse was,

he said "I am the one who spoke to you, the one you came to seek."

Puzzled, Mouse asked, "You, a butte, are talking to me?"

"Yes, it's me," the Butte replied. "You must be tired. Why don't you sit down and rest for a while? Have you perhaps come here for a special reason?"

"Yes, I have," Mouse replied. "I have a daughter who is old enough to marry, and I am out searching for a husband for her." He then proceeded to tell the Butte all about his daughter's qualities. "I think you can understand that I want only the best for such a girl."

Mouse also then related to the Butte how he had gone out seeking a husband, first going East to the Sun, then West to the Clouds, and finally to the cold North Winds. "According to the North Winds, it is you that no one can overpower. Therefore, I believe it is you who should marry my daughter."

Butte replied, "How fortunate for you to have such a daughter. But I must tell you that I too am not invincible. As a matter of fact, I'm not even a leader—I just stand

here, serving no purpose at all. The Sun beats down on me, the Clouds thunder and hurl their lightning and rain down on me and try to crack me apart. They pelt me with their flint weapons, but cannot penetrate me. The North Winds blow their hardest, trying to overturn me, but to no avail. None of these has been able to harm me. That may be why I'm regarded as superior to them all.

"But I'm really not the most powerful of all," the Butte continued. "I'll tell you why. It's because of you and your kind. Alone, you are tiny and insignificant, but I am convinced that a great number of you together could succeed in undermining me. Look at the numerous holes at my base, all leading to tunnels that extend throughout my entire body. All these were dug by you and your relatives, and when the rain comes, they become enlarged and sometimes collapse. If enough of you were to band together and dig thousands of these holes, I would surely be in grave danger of eroding completely away. Even though you are small and weak, you could conceivably bring me down. So don't waste your time traveling here and there, looking for a

husband, but return home and take a good look at the prospects there. Do the right thing and give your daughter to one of her own kind. I'm sure that together they will take good care of you and your wife."

Mouse agreed. "Yes, I will do that. I will go back home."

"Yes, that's right," the Butte repeated his advice, "don't waste your time looking for a son-in-law around here. Return to your home. You're bound to find someone suitable for your daughter there."

As he considered the Butte's last words, Mouse turned and headed for his home near Pavi'ovi. It was late evening when he arrived and was greeted by his daughter. "You are home to stay?"

"Yes," he replied.

"I am thankful that you are home," she said. "I've just finished making supper. Will you have some?"

"Yes," answered Mouse. He could see that his daughter and wife were happy to have him back. His daughter set out the food and while they were all eating, she said, "Father?"

"Yes," he replied.

"Remember when you departed for the East? You said that you were going to search for a husband for me. What did you find?"

"Well," began Mouse. "As you said, I first headed toward the East, in search of the Sun's home. He was the first one to whom I related the purpose of my journey. After all, it is he who travels the sky above us, giving us his heat. But when I made my proposal to him, he denied that he was first among all, and sent me West to the Clouds at Nuvatukya'ovi, saying that they ranked above him, as they had the power to blot him out when they gathered to rain.

"When I arrived at Nuvatukya'ovi, the Cloud chief, the eldest among them, conceded that when they gathered to make rain, they sometimes blocked out the Sun, and that in this way they could be considered more powerful. But he also said that in reality the Clouds and the Sun cooperated in producing the rain and the heat that together cause the crops to grow, the grasses to become beautifully green, and the land to burst out in flowers of all colors. And besides, the Cloud chief told me, 'There are those who

43

are more powerful than we—the North Winds—and they can blow us away at will.'

"Although I didn't really like the idea of one of the North Winds marrying my daughter, I went to see them as the Cloud chief suggested. A little halfheartedly I told them about you, and explained to them why I was there. Again, even these cold and wild North Winds admitted that they did not exceed all others, that there was one—the Butte— against which their powers were useless. Blow as they might, they could not affect him at all. So they sent me South to find him.

"When I arrived at the buttes south of Songoopavi, I saw no one to speak to, but after a while the Butte spoke to me and I told him why I had come. Although he admitted that neither the Sun with its heat; the Clouds with their lightning, rain, and hail; nor the howling North Winds had ever harmed him in the slightest, he denied being the highest in rank. He convinced me not to travel here and there looking for a husband for you, but to return home and seek one of our own kind for you." This is what Mouse related

to his daughter and wife about his travels and what he had learned.

"When the Butte told me why I should give up my search and return home, I was convinced. He showed me all the holes in his base and made me realize that we mice are possibly the only ones that have the power to destroy him. So I took the Butte's advice and here I am back home, without a husband for you. Now I think we must look for a suitable husband from among the youths that live here at Pavi'ovi."

"That's fine," his daughter acknowledged. "I'm glad to hear that. I know you wanted someone of great importance for me, but I really didn't want to marry a stranger. Anyone will do, even someone ordinary. As long as he works hard, I'm sure we'll survive."

"I understand," said Mouse. "The same thought occurred to me on the way home. I had in mind a youth who lives west of our place."

"Well then," said his daughter. "It is all right with me if you visit his parents and ask their permission. Of course, you should also ask the youth how he feels about this idea.

45

If they are all willing, I will marry him."

"All right," Mouse agreed. "I will visit them right after supper." After he had finished eating, he headed straight for the youth's home. When he reached there, he went right in, where he was greeted by the youth's father and the rest of the family. "I see you are out and about. Have a seat and stay a while. I expect that you have a good reason for coming."

"Yes, I do," replied Mouse. "I have a daughter, if you recall."

"Of course, we remember," they all said.

"Yes, and you may have heard that she knows how to do all sorts of things. She takes very good care of us. But my wife and I are getting on in years, and we would like for her to find a husband. Then when we are old, together they can take care of us." Mouse then told the youth and his parents all the details of his search, how he had looked for someone of high rank, and what he had been told by the various beings he had visited.

"The last one I visited, the Butte, really opened my eyes to the truth. He advised me not to waste any more of my time roaming the land looking for a husband, but to return home and give my daughter to one of her own kind. I took his advice to heart, and on the way home I remembered your son. I decided that he and my daughter would make a good match. This is my reason for coming to you now.

"I know you have many sons and daughters, and that there is still one son who is unmarried, the one who is sitting right here with us. I'm quite familiar with his habits and know he is of good character. I'm sure he's very industrious, because I often see him going out to your field with you. So that's really why I'm here, and I wonder what you have to say to that."

The youth's father replied, "Thank you very much indeed for the offer. But naturally, it's up to my son here. I'm only his father. If he agrees, I'm sure that together your daughter and my son will tend very well to your needs."

48

With that, he turned to his son and asked, "Do you want to marry this girl?"

"It's up to you, Father. If you're willing to weave the wedding garments for her, then I will go and live with her as her husband. I am perfectly willing to take care of her parents in their old age. I am not afraid to work hard and do everything necessary to raise enough food for us all, so I'm sure we'll all be able to survive."

When Mouse heard this, he was overjoyed. "Very well, thank you! By all means, marry her!"

And so Mouse and the youth left immediately for his home, where he presented the youth to his daughter. "All right, here is the youth that I spoke of. I have brought him for you. He is to be your husband."

"I see," said the daughter. "That is fine with me. I am sure he desires me and is willing to have me for his wife, for he came with you of his own accord. Together we will all live here, and when you have reached your old age, we'll take care of you, and of his mother and father as well."

49

51

This is how Mouse found a husband for his daughter.
The youth married her and settled down to a quiet life
of work and marriage. Each fall he would harvest his crops
and provide for his in-laws as well as his own parents. The
mouse couple felt happy and secure because they knew that
someone would care for them when they became old
and helpless. And so they all lived there together, enjoying
life to its fullest. Perhaps they still live there near Pavi'ovi.
And here the story ends.

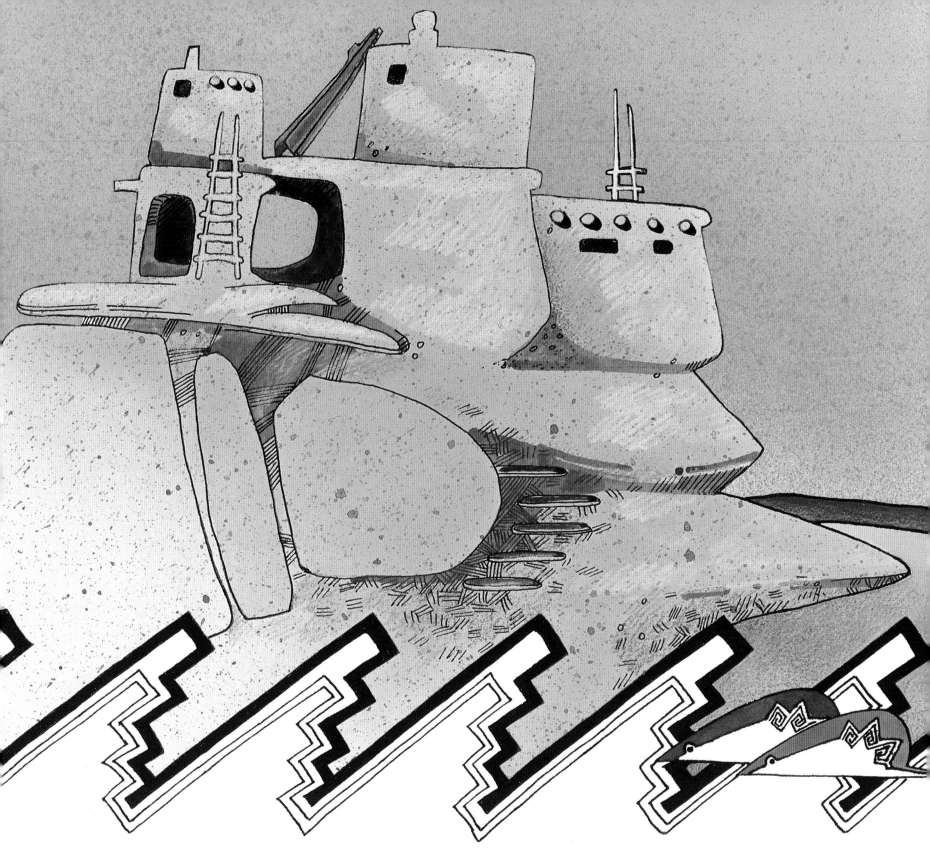

Afterword

The objective of this book is two-fold. First, it preserves an authentic folktale in an age when not only is the art of storytelling sharply declining throughout the world, but whole bodies of oral tradition are vanishing into oblivion. Second, it attempts to fill a perceived void in the availability of quality children's literature based on ethnic sources.

At a time when multicultural views and values are receiving ever-increasing attention and significance in society, the nearly total absence of quality children's literature is most disconcerting. To be sure, American Indian "kiddie stories" abound. Generally, however, they represent either watered-down plot capsules of original native tales or are written by cultural outsiders with artificial injections of supposed "Indian" flavor. These texts tend to be condescending and this problem is compounded by the often-cartoonish illustrations.

Mouse Couple tries to avoid these pitfalls. While I regret that, in the format of this children's book, the Hopi original could not appear side-by-side with the English rendition, the tale nevertheless constitutes a faithful sample of Hopi oral literature. *Pösnawuutim*, the Hopi version, was related to me in 1983 by Sidney Namingha Jr., not long before his tragic and untimely death. He deserves all of the credit for remembering this wonderful story. Michael Lacapa's artwork makes the transition from live storyteller to printed page possible. Working on this challenge with Michael was a delight and I am deeply grateful to him for the enthusiasm he displayed toward the task of capturing the essence of the story in culturally relevant imagery. Finally, I need to thank my friend Ken Gary for polishing the manuscript stylistically. With his admirable gift for writing and his sensitive empathy for the Hopi culture, he has once again greatly improved the readability of my translation.

E. M.

EKKEHART MALOTKI is a philologist and linguist who received his PhD in 1976. Currently he is professor of languages at Northern Arizona University where he teaches German. His entire research is devoted to analyzing and preserving Hopi language and culture; he has collected hundreds of narratives in the course of his field work. Of the eight bilingual books he has published, two have won awards. He is a principal investigator for the comprehensive Hopi-English dictionary project, funded by the National Endowment for the Humanities.

MICHAEL LACAPA, who is of Apache/Hopi/Tewa descent, is trained both as an illustrator and as an artist. In addition to participating in numerous one-man and group exhibitions, he has served as artist-in-residence for several Arizona schools. Lacapa's work combines references from his cultural background with sophisticated and stylized line and color into a distinctive artistic statement.